SCI-FI - SERIES I

Thirsty Work is absolutely hilarious!
A weird and twisty tale the likes I have not seen in
many a year. Reminds me of Ray Bradbury's early
work before he got all dark and serious...

Thaddeus Howze, author, San Francisco, USA

"Absolutely brilliant!
I so enjoyed reading this short story, written with
great wit and imagination.
A real classic, which leaves the reader wondering if
we do really live on Planet Earth!"

Louisa Middleton-Blake, author, Wales, UK.

Sci-Fi Series 1

Anthology of Short Stories

Stan I.S. Law

Published by
INHOUSEPRESS

CONTENTS

Thirsty Work

Ah, thank you kindly, bartender. Much appreciated. Cheers!

So when they accused me of being inebriated, *me*, who wouldn't even inhale the fumes while piloting my hopper, I simply told them the truth:

No, Sir, I said. I took every precaution possible. I even posted beacons.

They said: Your objection is noted. Nevertheless, a three-month suspension is upheld by this court.

And that was that. And just how am I supposed to make a living in the meantime? Guys like me don't retire. We work or we starve. Except for what we can scrounge and then multiply. But you've got to scrounge it first, right? Anyway, to start with, it wasn't my fault. Sure my ship was invisible, but not to their radar. And I made doubly sure they already had radar. For years, now. How would I know that they would ignore it?

Thank you, barman. To your very good health, too!

How did it all start, you ask? Would you believe it even if I told you? O.K..

Listen to this...

Three months ago, I found this little planet. It looked cute from up above. Nice and blue with pretty little cloud patches scattered haphazardly, but still, it made a friendly impression on me. It looked like I might be able to do a little business down there. I'm a trader, by trade. I like to do a little business. Even with primitives. Why not? You never know until you try. If both parties make a profit, what's the harm in that?

I left my cruiser on their cute little moon (didn't want to show off, you understand?) and took my hopper down to the surface. I had no idea what they might have to offer. It would have taken some research, and I was feeling tired. Fifty light-years takes a lot of Umph out of you. I needed to rest.

As I already told you, I checked on their technology, found out they used radar, so I set beacons, just to be doubly safe, you understand, and went to sleep. I made the hopper invisible, of course.

For all I knew, they could have started shooting at me. I might have been trespassing or something. Don't forget, I had no idea if the natives were friendly, or not. I can see through most solids, but I am not a mind reader.

I'd hardly closed my eyes when the alarms started making a racket like you wouldn't believe. They went absolutely frantic. I spread myself across the whole cabin. My hopper viewers told the whole story! I had one blithering idiot coming straight at me. A winged craft full of Umph on my left, another on my right, and listen to this, another straight above. If I'd made a run for it, the turbulence would've squeezed them all out of their skins. So what the hell would you do? There was no way to go but down, (and that's when my real problems started!). I sat, I mean landed, right on top of him!

He was just standing there, in the middle of an open field. What would anybody, even a primitive, be doing in an open field was beyond me. He seemed to be picking something up from the soil. How was I to know they didn't even have food synthesizers down there yet? I mean, I ask you. Would you have guessed? Have *you* ever seen a Xeno in an open field? So there you are.

Anyway, I sat on him. Only then I found out he had Umph. I can read a group of them from a distance, but a single native down there, has so little Umph it's hard to read from any distance. Only he was losing it fast. I did the only thing possible. I grounded the hopper, oozed out in a split second and grabbed his mould with all I had. In a few seconds, I looked exactly like the fellow. About five foot nine, half-bald, rather craggy, dumb looking face and, I later learned, 'bout sixty. Imagine, I killed a juvenile! I'm telling you, it just didn't feel good.

I stood there, scratching my head (they seem to do that there when they don't know what to do), and then an awful sound shot through my ears:

"Joshua! Come here! How long does it take to pick enough potatoes for supper?"

As I was saying. That voice wasn't a nice sound.

I looked around me. Now listen to this. I picked up most of the memories this Joshua had before his Umph left him completely. There is a thing they call a brain, down there. Or should I say, up there? Anyway, it's not a bad memory storage device. Once you learn to use it, it's not that bad. The funny thing is, I found out later, most of them don't use it at all. Ever! Well, hardly ever, for all I could see.

So I looked around, picked up their 'potatoes', and carried them to the house. That was my second shock. My God, was she ugly! She was the ugliest woman I have ever smelled. I didn't know such people still existed in the Galaxy. You could, literarily, smell her character within a couple of light years. No, really. I hadn't spotted her immediately only because I'd been so preoccupied with sitting on Joshua. Wouldn't you be? You know what the Law says about displacing someone's Umph without permission? I was dead scared I would lose my license permanently. I closed my nose and handed her the potatoes. What do you think she said? Thank you? Hah!

She said: "You're too slow, Joshua. Next time I'll get them myself and you can make your own supper." That was the thanks I got for her stupid potatoes. I am telling you, talk of a primitive!

Joshua and the uglie, whose name, by the way, was Harrietta, lived out in the countryside. They operated a gas station and grew their own vegetables. Harrietta, or Harriet, was supposed to look after the vegetables and Joshua after the gas.

What's gas? Well, it's not easy to tell. It's a foul-smelling liquid they use to propel rusting boxes of metal and plastic along the ground. They move along, as slowly as an ageing Gimmean snail, on wheels. No, don't laugh. I'm serious. On four, round wheels! The boxes are called automobiles. But they are auto-nothing. Without this gas, they don't get anywhere. I'm telling you, it's weird!

But let's get back to the story.

This Harriet woman was a monster. Whatever Joshua did, it was either wrong, or too slow, or too low, or too high. I'm telling you, she was a real Yahoo. They have some in a zoo on Quaqq, but here, or rather there, she was a live one, *and* walking around without a leash. Would you believe it?

I had to find a way out of this mess. My hopper was grounded out in the field, invisible of course, but sooner or later Harriet would bump her ugly face on it and Joshua, that's me don't forget, would get it again. On top of that, the hopper had the right recto-boosters bent, and it has been a while since I moulded one. I needed time to do the repairs.

In the meantime, I had no choice but to take Joshua's place. It wasn't easy. The automobiles kept pulling up at the gas station and I had to fill their tanks with the propellant. That alone left me with very little free time. Once I got the know-how about their mode of travel, I managed to get rid of most of my customers. At least the local ones. I simply adapted the gas molecules to keep exfoliating themselves, in liquid layers, so as to keep their fuel tanks full. So after that, these clients never came again. It got Harriet grumbling that we weren't making any money, but it gave me more time to mould my own repairs. What would you have done?

Sooner or later I had to get away from the Uglie or go mad. Also, I couldn't stay forever in Joshua's body. For all I knew it might disintegrate one day. I already felt strange aches and pains. What's what? Aches and pains? That's when your body tells you about the things you did wrong before. It's a crazy way to learn, but apparently, even this method didn't do the natives much good.

I'm telling you, the Yahoo was driving me nuts. She said that now that we had fewer customers, I could do more in the field. You know, potatoes and such like. Well, there was a plus side to this. It kept Harriet away from my hopper, and it kept me close to it. Who said there is no justice?

Now and again, she would call me to the garage.

"Joshuaaaa!" she would holler. "Get your lazy ass here. Customers are waiting. I can't do everything myself, can I!?"

Boy, I could tell her!

Everything herself? Like cooking the foul tasting slop they use for food there? I don't wish it on my worst enemy, with the possible exception of the Boohoos who did me out of a fair profit last year. Anyway, I'd go to the garage, fill their tank once and for all, and go back to my hopper. It's not easy trying to mould complex shapes with constant interruptions. On the other hand, once I was in the garage, I could keep trying out new ideas. Sometimes I would fit the customers with new tires. They used rubber rims over metal wheels, which would wear out in no time at all. Instead, I fitted them a mould into which the tires continued to expand. Why not? Who wants to change tires every couple of years?

You see, after only a week or two, I thought I was beginning to think like some of the natives. Only I was wrong! In fact, their whole economy is based on obsolescence. If something works, they change it to make it worse. Mind you, that's the only way they manage to keep people employed. I'm telling you... The chief people in charge of obsolescence are called politicians. They create policies to keep people as dumb as possible by making decisions for them. You know—making sure people don't start thinking for themselves. That way, the masses are easier to control.

Control for what? How the devil do I know? Most people I met were happiest when they were doing nothing. So what is there to control?

Anyway, this dragged on for a couple of months. That's about two galactic ticks. My booster moulds were coming along very nicely, thank you, but I had very little time to work on them. After all, how often do you repair your boosters? I almost forgot their precise moulds. I've been using the same ones for the last million years. Light-years. Unless you sit on someone, these moulds last forever. It was the Umph that did the damage.

Yes, barman, I will have another one. Thank you. Yea, it sure is thirsty work. Here's to you. Cheers, and all that!

Anyway, then I got lucky.

We were sitting at the dinner table, Harriet and I, eating. I liked those moments, even if the food was lousy. Why? Because the Uglie couldn't talk with her mouth stuffed to the brim. Once the meal was over, she started yapping again. After a while, just this once, I started to listen.

After the usual half-hour nagging about this, that and the other, or whatever, she was now going on and on about the goldfish. There was this fair size glass bowl, filled with water, some weeds, a few pebbles, and a solitary goldfish. She started yapping about how the goldfish had been lonely, that her own life hadn't amounted to anything, that she, herself, was like this poor, lonely goldfish, all closed off in the middle of nowhere. Then she ended up by saying that she's in a goldfish prison because I never take her anywhere.

Then she really poured her guts out. She might as well live in the bowl herself, she said. At least then, neither of them would be alone. She said she might as well *be* a goldfish. Since I weren't any company for her, she said, at least she and the goldfish would swim there together. Why not, she asked? And without waiting for an answer she said that I never even talked to her.

Now that wasn't quite true. Only a week earlier I had told her to shut up or... I forget exactly what my inspiration was at the time. It was a phrase I picked up from a customer in the garage. Something about rearranging her brains in her thinkbox. But that wasn't the point! You know about the rules. We're not allowed to put anyone anywhere, without their permission. And here she was, practically begging me, to stick her in the bowl. Now, I ask you. Would you refuse to make the Uglie happy? According to her, for the first time in her miserable life?

Not me. All my customers, throughout the galaxy, know me to be of a generous, you might even say, magnanimous, disposition. No, really. You don't have to ask me twice. Before she could change her mind, I studied the mould of the lone goldfish, then took one look at Harriet, her mouth still open, and, there she was. Swimming around as if she'd been practicing all her life. For a moment I thought she might sink, with all that ballast, but then I saw that Harriet had always been some ninety-six percent water. Now, wasn't that lucky?

My God, it got quiet in the house.

Now with Harriet's mouth opening and closing but no sound coming out, I could have stayed there another tick or two. But it so happened that the next day I hit the right mould for my boosters. Frankly, by that time, I had lost hope that I could make a good trade on that planet. Oh, don't get me wrong. The natives had some marvellous ideas. Their imagination is as good as any I've felt within the Matrix, but... well, how could I reciprocate? The only moulds I had would last for thousands of years. That would upset their whole economy. Whatever moulds their produce themselves, with their imagination, they make sure that the product falls apart in no time at all. And if it is more sturdy, then they manufacture a thing they call pollution. That is a complex substance, which they discharge into their air, water, and even bury it in their soil, so that the acids, and such like, eat into their ideas. I'm telling you. They live in a garbage dump. And the view from the moon looks so nice. So green and blue, and peaceful...

To each his own. Right? Yes, thank you, barman. I will. You're a man after my own heart. Cheers.

So anyway, I couldn't possibly leave Harriet behind in the fishbowl with the other fish. I could try and make a mould to feed her, but it's more complex than that. Would you believe that they don't absorb

all their food down there? They shove enormous
amounts of it into their distended stomachs, and then,
listen to this, they get rid of most of it from their
other ends. Evil smelling stuff, too. What a waste!

Anyway, with my boosters ready, I took the
fishbowl with me to my hopper, secured it with some
good ideas, and off we went. Harriet still continued to
keep her mouth open, but she couldn't complain
aloud, anymore. So why not take her with me?
Before taking off, I reverted back to my standard
navigational shape. With twenty-seven controls,
twenty-seven appendages seemed appropriate. Once I
was up in the air, I looked at the fishbowl to make
sure Harriet was all right. Now the funniest thing
happened. She took one look at me and turned belly
up. Literarily, upside down! The next thing I heard
was her Umph splitting. It left her so quickly you
could actually hear it!

So what would you do? I absorbed her. That
way, she and Joshua could be together again. Within
me, so to speak. Only I'm still not sure that Joshua
would have wanted it this way. Well, at least his
Umph was free, and the rest was mostly water
anyway.

That's 'bout it, barman. Tomorrow I'm getting
my license back. I'm going back to work. Got to do
something. I feel like making some really good

moulds. My imagination's been itching for three months now.

So long, then. I owe you one. What? I owe you six? Well, a figure of speech. My other appendages? You mean thirty-six. Well, with six mouths, it seemed appropriate. Anyway, put it on my tab. O.K.?

Name? *My* name? Oh, for the tab. Sure. Only you can't really say it. You've got to, sort of, sing it. Like this: Ooohyeea! On three different notes. Go on, give it a try.

Ooohyeea!?

There, you got it. First time, too. You must have heard it before. People often give me credit when credit is due. They often mention my name when they get a really good mould. It's like a referral. In all humility, there's a chance, probably two to one, that I had something to do with it. Are you a betting man, barman?

Pity.

Say, you wouldn't like to trade that ale for a nice barrel mould? It would stay full forever. You would? O.K., then. Only I have to remind you, moulding is very thirsty work.

***

The Acorn

The queue was at least a mile long. People did not seem to mind. The temperature, perhaps a little too hot even for late summer, made waiting seem part of the holiday. Year after year, on both days of the Unification Holiday, lines had formed, orderly, resounding with the clutter of excited children. Many of them were visiting the arboretum for the very first time.

"Are there many trees, daddy? Really many, many trees? Like in a forest?" Jenny asked, tugging at Paul's hand, unwilling to wait and find out for herself. She knew about the forest from a book on the history of the American Federation her older brother had shown her.

"Yes, dear. There are many trees. All different kinds."

Paul Brady was busy scanning the market report he had to analyze for Monday. He could ill afford to miss a whole day of work. Even on a weekend. He could work while the queue made its snail-paced advance towards the air-lock. Once there, the guards would allow up to one hundred people, simultaneously, into the protective chamber but only after an equal number had left at the other end of the air control passage. Later, once inside the arboretum proper, the procession of people, mostly parents conducting their children, would move slowly along a winding, raised platform. Sometimes the platform sloped upwards, bridging a tiny stream or rising up and over some manmade rocky mounds. When on such bridges, one could be within five or six feet of the lowest branches. Such closeness to the trees, to things green and growing, would be quite thrilling. Even for Paul who still held on to dim memories of the dying, defoliated stubs of trees in what once had been the Municipal Park on the outskirts of town. Memories that took him back to his own childhood. To when he had been not much older than Jenny was now.

"Come on daddy. We'll lose our place!" Jenny tugged on Paul's sleeve again.

Jenny was his youngest. In fact, she was not a 'planned' child. Not in accordance with the latest Federal Family Planning recommendations. The Policy was quite direct and simple: People created pollution. Reduce the number of people and you reduce pollution. If you could not reduce the number of people, then at least reduce their income. Less income, less pollution.

The logic of survival.

Paul and Ann Brady had been paying five percent of their combined income to offset the pollution to which little Jenny would eventually contribute. Five percent of their income for twenty years of their working lives. It would have been a lot worse if they had twins again. The fourth child would have meant a ten percent penalty. That, added to five, would greatly affect their standard of living. They would have to move to the left bank where the larger families lived. Vegetated. Nobody from the left bank could possibly afford the entrance fee to the arboretum. Not for any of their children.

Paul remembered when he and his wife had taken the twins to the great dome. Thirteen years ago. Eighteen years after the last tree had officially died. Paul had read, somewhere, that trees had started dying in the middle of the last century. Some of the perennials seemed to have adapted. Trees hadn't. It had been an uneven battle. Early this century, the only forests that remained were the proud, soaring stacks of industrial chimneys. They stood out boldly against a yellowish-grey sky, lonely, indifferent.

Necessary. Below them, at the human level, machines manufactured proteins, starch, suchlike, to make up for the barren fields.

Food substitutes. Chemicals.

Then came the earthquakes. Not great or cataclysmic. Just enough to stir the bowels, deep down. To open up nature's chimneys, the long-dormant volcanoes. Thousands of them. The experts blamed it all on planetary alignments, on unpropitious convergence of their orbits, on the sunspot activity, on the melting polar icecaps, on anything they could think of. It did not really matter. The rains that followed carried ash, suphur, hydrocarbons and God knows what other poisons. Within five years the deciduous, then coniferous trees, gave in to the noxious slime.

"Move along now, please. Please form a single file," the speaker announced.

Once inside, the queue would widen to two, side by side. For now, Paul let go Jenny's hand and stood behind her. Again Paul thought of his last visit here. With the twins. Now George and Peter lived on their own. Paul felt a gentle thrill of anticipation. Would he remember the names of some of the more common trees? He closed his eyes trying to visualize them. Only one form came to mind: the oak.

The oak had been the king of trees. It had been

august, majestic.

There were now only about forty people in the queue in front of Paul and Jenny. They were bound to get in at the next change over. Paul raised his mask and took a deep drag on the plastic tube. The oxygen felt good. Necessary. They had been outdoors now for almost two hours. Too long. Once inside, at least for a while, they would enjoy a climate of eternal spring. Filled with air. Real, breathable air. No filtering masks would be required. They could even leave their oxygen tanks at the doors, although that would be risky. Things got stolen.

Once inside, it would feel like being at home only the *impression* would be that of being outdoors. A closed, controlled environment. It had to be. For the lawns, flowers, small bushes. And, of course, the trees.

Children would discover that the myth about the majestic trees was not really a myth. Trees had really existed. Once. The world over. Jenny would look, absorb and arrange it all neatly in her receptive, voracious mind. Or look, smile and place it side by side with other myths; side by side with Santa Clause, the Tooth Fairy, the Man-on-the-Moon and many other dreams and images, passing, ephemeral, yet vital to preserve a sane, balanced mind in this warped, perennially insane world. Later, as she grew, the myth would fail. Even as the last trees had. Irrevocably.

But not today.

Today was a day of celebration. A toast to our past, to dark, mysterious forests. Jenny would learn about the large expanse of land which had stretched, once, across vast continents, from one ocean to another, all green and luscious. Today, those images would be on screens throughout the walk. Paul remembered how impressed he had been by them. The pictures were *almost* real. He could still smell them. Jenny would also see images of countless wild animals, birds which lived and lurked and fed and frolicked, unimpeded by man, quite freely, in the mysterious innards of the verdant groves, thickets and profuse woodlands. Those were images she would not easily forget. The entry ticket would be worth every dollar, even if it meant no wine on the dinner table for a month or so.

"The first sixty people advance to the front please," the speaker commanded.

Paul kept his hand on Jenny's head, just to make sure. She couldn't get lost – she was wearing her new pink hat bought especially for their trip to the arboretum – but... you never know. Children were an expensive commodity. One learned to be protective of them. Perhaps, a little more than when he was young. Nowadays they needed just that extra little care. There were so few things the kids could do. Like playing outside for more than an hour daily. And even then he, or Ann, would have to change the filter in Jenny's mask at least every second day. The children deserved a little more protection.

Jenny walked forward, anxious to push through with the other children, to finally get inside. Paul and the other parents followed his emotions again taking him back to the last visit. My God, he thought. So many trees. So many....

At last, they were inside a large room. Quickly, the parents and children got seated, side by side in an open, Disney-World-type railway car. Children scrambled for the best seats, those close to the edge. Then the train moved off, drawing them into a dark tunnel. Gentle, soothing music, gradually gave way to strange sounds. When their eyes adjusted to the dim surroundings, Jenny was the first to notice peculiar, closely spaced points of light in the forbidding darkness. She leaned closer to her father, firmly grabbing his arm. Unknown beasts followed her from the dark. As the train advanced, dim, seeping light slowly exposed them to the innards of deep, mysterious jungle.

Paul loved this effect. It really did look as if they were crossing an impenetrable jungle. The thick, powerful branches, entwined and twisted with convoluted liana, created a most frightening yet exhilarating effect. Even the air was heavy with humidity, filled with buzzing, humming noises. Now and then a bloody shriek would cut the shadows, then whimper into dark-green oblivion. Now both Jenny's arms held tight to Paul's arm. It seemed a long time before the light dissipated the dark images. The train deposited them in the arboretum proper. The long jungle air-lock was behind them.

The masks were removed.

The whole visit would last exactly four hours. The moment they stepped off the train, a pretty, uniformed guide approached Paul. She smiled a plastic smile and asked if Paul would like a guided tour. Paul could ill-afford one. There were hundreds of trees up ahead. Hundreds. What the hell! Once every thirteen years. Paul felt strangely elated.

Intoxicated.

The moment Delta, the guide, punched Paul's card for the requisite credits, she took them to one side. Immediately she began giving Jenny a carefully structured discourse on the various types of trees. The other visitors walked in small groups, some with guides, some without, stopping on some raised sidewalks, to ask questions, or to admire a particularly beautiful exhibit. And trees were everywhere. Masses and masses of them. The geodesic dome enclosing the whole installation measured over twelve hundred meters in diameter and a good hundred meters high. The walkway climbed little hills, descended into open glades nestling in secluded valleys, then turning suddenly to present them with a new, magnificent vista. Jenny saw clumps of trees against the background of a distant forest. The fact that this distant forest had been painted onto the wall didn't really matter.

Sheer beauty.

The visit to the arboretum had been planned for Jenny, but Ann insisted she and Paul draw straws to decide who would have the privilege of taking her.

Paul won. Now, he could not hide his joy at the sight of his own parents' childhood. His obstinate heart refused to accept that the images he now witnessed were not real. It was the Outside which, surely, was a bad dream. Here, this was the reality, the beauty captured in the books he had read, in the dreams he still dreamed.

When they reached a raised platform, Delta excused herself to walk over and politely remind some other guests to stay on the path.

"Really…" she sighed, "why must people touch things? Don't they understand how delicate this ecosystem is?"

Paul took Jenny to one side of the walkway, to let others pass. Jenny, her eyes bright with wonder, leaned over the railing. Paul understood. She wanted to be closer to a particularly beautiful, nameless bush, resplendent in full bloom. As she leaned over, something dropped on her head. It got caught in the upturned brim of her hat. Jenny reached up carefully, curious about the offending object. It was a greenish-brown acorn. An acorn just reaching its maturity.

"Daddy, daddy, look daddy!" Jenny danced with joy. "Oh daddy, I can keep it, can I. Oh, daddy, can I?" Her eyes flicked between the acorn and Paul's face.

Paul knew the rules. Visitors were not allowed to pick *any* living flora and take it with them to the outside. But was the acorn living? And after all, had anyone picked it? It had dropped from the wide oak, above them. Surely, that's not picking.

"Put it in your pocket and do not take it out until we get home. All right?" He said gently, but his face discouraged disobedience. Jenny had no desire to argue. She secreted the acorn in the deep pocket of the pleated skirt and turned her attention to the returning guide.

"What is this tree above us?" Jenny asked tossing her head backwards and pointing up with both hands.

"That is the king of all trees, dear. It is called an oak tree." It was evident that the guide was enjoying her work. The original plastic smile had softened to sincerity.

Jenny seemed to consider this for a while. Then her eyes lit up as though struck by a sudden thought.

"How do oak trees have babies?" She asked. Paul was ready to silence his inquisitive daughter, but the guide gently restrained him. The fact that Jenny had probably no clear idea of how people have children did not have to have any bearing on this.

"Well, let me see, now. Once a year the oak tree has flowers. The flowers, inside their cups, have a powder called pollen. When an insect sits on a flower, some of the pollen settles on its legs. Then the insect flies away and sits on another oak tree flower, and the two pollen get mixed together. Then, in time, a seed is grown from the flower. It is called an acorn. When the acorn falls down to the ground, it too can become an oak tree." Delta did her best. She obviously was much too young to ever have seen any of it happen.

"What's an insect?" Jenny asked.

"I'll explain it to you at home, Jenny." Paul stepped in. They had only a little over an hour left and there was still the three-hundred-sixty-degree film theatre to see. He wanted to make the most of the remaining time. Jenny changed her tactics.

"And the acorn just lies there? On the ground?" She persisted.

"Well, it should be covered with a little earth, and then it needs some water. And then..."

"Common Jenny, let's see the rest of the arboretum," Paul cut in.

They had to practically jog through the subtropical section to make it to the theatre without paying for another shift. John would have gladly stayed on, but it would not be fair to Ann. If Jenny were to visit the arboretum again, it would be with his wife. Anyway, Jenny seemed quite content. She didn't ask any more questions, but through the rest of the visit, her face seemed held in rapt attention. On the way home, Jenny didn't say a single word. She seemed lost in her thoughts. Paul did not interrupt her. He had his own memories to ponder.

A few days later, Jenny asked Paul about babies. About the *making* of babies. Paul sent her to her mother. Jenny was back within an hour, flustered.

"Mummy told me only about the boy children and the girl children." Her face was a study of profound disappointment. "I want to know about acorns."

Paul remembered the object landing on Jenny's

head in the arboretum. He smiled at the recollection.
"And what have you done with it?" He asked his
frazzled daughter.

"I did what Delta told me. And I have seen no
babies." Her face was becoming more unhappy. "And
I water it daily, just like she told me."

Paul remembered Jenny's studious silence on the
way home from the arboretum. Now it seemed
obvious that she had decided, there and then, to
rebuild the continents of missing forests. She was
much too young to partake in the racial guilt for their
disappearance. The blame which every day seemed
to hover at the edge of Paul's own awareness. Like
the original sin.

"It takes time, darling. A long, long time.
Sometimes a whole winter, before an acorn can have
babies. I mean, before an acorn grows into a baby, a
tiny tree." Paul said sadly. How could he tell his own
sweet daughter that the acorn couldn't possibly grow
into a tree in their polluted soil? Even if it did
germinate, it would die long before it could become
even a seedling. His one hope was that, come
springtime, Jenny would forget all about it.

And then springtime came.

"Oh daddy, daddy!" Jenny ran in from the paved
'garden', immediately tugging on Paul's sleeve. Her

voice was muffled by her mask. She was six now. Her tugging was a lot more persuasive.

"What is it, dear?" Paul asked still hoping to be left alone. He had to spend four hours outdoors today. Prolonged breathing through the mask always left him tired.

"Come with me, daddy. Please come!" Jenny was almost frantic.

Paul sighed resignedly. He pushed himself up from a deep armchair, away from his favourite book. He followed Jenny into their garden. Strange how names persist. There wasn't a single plant in the backyard. The outdoor space served no other purpose than to separate him and his family from their neighbours. It was a visual barrier filled with rocks, sand, and some decorative paving. Something to rest his eyes on after spending a whole day in an office cubicle.

Jenny, still maintaining a firm hold on his sleeve, led him to the fence. There, some of the decorative, multicoloured pebbles had been carefully piled to one side, exposing a circle of brownish soil. In the very center of the circle, no more than a foot high, was a perfectly healthy-looking little oak tree.

Paul blinked hard. This could not possibly have happened. For years now, the scientists had been trying, quite unsuccessfully, to test new, chemically 'repaired' soils. Even when seedlings had been transplanted from protected, indoor environments, they had died after a single season. This acorn had survived a fall and a winter. *This just could not be.* Yet he was seeing it with his own eyes.

"When did this happen?" Paul asked, his voice a little husky. He hadn't bothered with his mask and the smog affected his throat immediately.

"Until yesterday it was only a stick with little bumps. But today it has leaves on!" Jenny, her eyes filled with joy, clapped her hands together.

This was much too big for Paul to handle himself. He discussed it with his wife. They examined the seedling for two weeks, before and after work. It grew with all the joys of spring. Then, for two weeks, every two days, they took a series of photographs. There were small but discernible differences in the sequential photos. After three weeks, Paul went to see the public relations officer at the arboretum. He had made an appointment.

Mr. Jason McBride, a polished looking gentleman with just enough grey at the temples to give him an air of quiet distinction, offered his gloved hand.

"Security..." he murmured pointing at the gloves apologetically, "germs and all that." Paul understood.

A single germ might destroy the whole tree collection. All people in the arboretum wore gloves.

McBride asked Paul to sit down. Paul was nervous. Rather than attempting a long introduction, Paul reached into his breast pocket and took out the photographs. He put them on the large mahogany desk. Then, thankfully, words came at a flood. Paul described what had happened. He said he knew it was illegal to pick anything in the arboretum, but this acorn had actually fallen on Jenny's head. Hat. They had not picked it. And surely, it had not been alive. I mean, surely, not really.... Paul concluded. Then Paul wished he had asked for some water.

The distinguished Mr. McBride listened without a single interruption. When Paul had finished, Mr. McBride looked at the photographs, smiled, and looked up. Seeing Paul's agitated condition, he poured some water into Paul's glass and placed it before his guest.

"That is quite right, Mr. Brady. It is a lovely story. Your daughter must like it very much. And the seedlings are superbly made." His features reflected professional admiration.

"What is quite right?" Paul gulped some water. He had no idea what Mr. McBride was saying. "What is quite right?" he repeated.

"You have said, Mr. Brady, that the acorn was

not alive. As such there is no liability on your part. You have not broken any laws." Jason McBride assured Paul with a broad, paternal smile. "But the seedlings are a work of a talented artist. We would certainly like to hear from him. Or is it her?" He beamed another smile.

They were talking at cross-purposes. Mr. McBride was talking about some artificial plant maker. What was the matter with him? Had he not listened to my story? Did I forget anything?

"Mr. McBride. You don't seem to understand me. The 'story', as you call it, which I have just told you is true. My daughter planted the acorn she brought from your arboretum in our garden, last summer. It survived the winter. And now it is a healthy, growing, oak tree. I think this should be reported to some authorities. Perhaps the soil in my garden has some special properties. Perhaps the acorns have become acclimatized to the acidity of the rain and soil. Perhaps..." Paul was interrupted by Mr. McBride's raised gloved hand.

"Perhaps, Mr. Brady. But you see, there is just one problem. Now, how shall I put it? We do not advertise what I am about to tell you. It is not a State Secret," Mr. McBride permitted himself a surreptitious chuckle, "but I will ask you for strict confidence. It would not be good for our image. You see, Mr. Brady, we have six hundred and eighty-two trees, in our arboretum. To maintain such a vast number of trees at the same level and quality as we do our lawns and flowering shrub, we would need a hundred times as much water, a hundred times as many staff, and even then, how would we remove the dead trees? It is not like cutting grass or placing a wilting bush on a wheelbarrow. Now is it?" Jason McBride was at his most persuasive.

Paul was beginning to suspect the impossible. "No, Mr. McBride. It isn't. So what are you driving at?" Paul refused to give way to his suspicions.

"So you see, Mr. Brady, while all the lawns, flowers and bushes are, ah, organic, the trees, for obvious reasons, economic mainly but also a hundred others, well, they are all made of plastic.

Paul cringed. He did not believe for a moment that the arboretum, where he had just paid practically a week's salary for one visit, would display plastic trees. He smiled with good humour.

"And I suppose, the acorns are made of plastic, too?" he asked.

"That is right, Mr. Brady. Rather well made, don't you think? Most people have forgotten what an acorn looks like but we still try to do the very best we can. And that is why we are always interested in finding new talent. Judging by these photos, whoever made these seedlings, is an excellent artist. Now tell me the truth, Mr. Brady. Don't be modest. It was your own work, wasn't it?" Mr. McBride, true to his word, was looking for new talent.

Paul gave in and played the game. "As a matter of fact, it was my daughter's."

"Really! How very precocious. You must promise to let me meet her. When she grows up a little, of course." Mr. McBride added.

Paul got up. He decided to go home and wait for some government official to contact him. It was evident that Mr. McBride was not free to speak to him openly. No matter. There was no real hurry. The two men shook hands and wished each other every success in the future.

Paul was quite flattered that Mr. McBride took him into his confidence, even if veiled and inverted. Such stories as plastic trees in the arboretum were obviously—just stories. One does not build a kilometer-sized dome to protect *artificial* trees. But Paul's, or Jenny's really, discovery of an acorn surviving two full seasons, in outdoor conditions, was of such magnitude that it had to be deferred to higher authorities. Obviously. On returning home, Paul swore Ann and Jenny to secrecy and they all decided to wait.

When Paul left his office, Mr. McBride grew

pensive. A single deep furrow formed in the middle of his otherwise perfectly smooth forehead. Jason McBride was worried. He glanced at his diary. Paul had been the third man this month. Down south it was even worse. The arboretum in New York had had six such cases this spring already. McBride knew that they could not maintain secrecy forever, but... it was still too early. They needed more time.

He pressed a button and spoke into the intercom. Then he sat back and waited. Jason McBride loved the arboretum, he loved his office, his work, but most of all he loved his desk. Its beautiful, richly grained surface, the depth of sheen greater, richer than any ordinary wood could ever aspire to. He shook his head. Pity, he murmured. He swung his armchair to face the window.

Soon there was a knock on his door.

"Yes, sir?" Delta stood nearly at attention.

McBride didn't move. He told her to sit and listen. He recounted the story Paul Brady had told him. He spoke slowly, choosing his words carefully. Then he swung his chair to face Delta.

"And just what the hell did you think you were doing when you told that little pip-squeak how oak trees have babies?" McBride regarded Delta with a stern, angry expression. He didn't wait for a reply. He was fuming mad. "Where does it say that the propagation of the species is part of the guide's curriculum?"

As her boss talked, Delta sat straight, almost rigid, silent, but her head progressively drooped towards her shiny, plastic shoes.

McBride did not expect an answer to any of his questions. "Here," he said. "Take it and do what is necessary."

Delta got up, took from Jason's desk Paul Brady's address and left the office. She was sorry for Jenny. Such a nice, pretty girl. What a pity. Still, it had to be done. It was a matter of survival.

Jason McBride sat back, calmer but still pensive. He wondered how long it could last. Sooner or later people would catch on. There were twenty-two thousand arboreta, worldwide. They were all run by men like him. Since his great-great-grandfather first succeeded in altering human DNA, introducing a new variant, the rest had been easy. In a way it was funny. He and such as himself were the only people capable of living and enjoying life on the outside of the arboretum. Yet they were the only ones who stayed in. At least during the daytime.

For countless generations man had spent billions of dollars attempting to change the environment to suit his needs. He ended up destroying it. Almost. How much simpler, how much sounder, ecologically, to adapt man to the environment?

It had taken a generation to replace most of the trees in the arboreta. It would take a lot longer to replace men.

On the first moonless night, Delta would run along and spray Jenny's poor little seedling with concentrated sulphuric acid. McBride smiled. *Concentrated*, he repeated in his thoughts. Nothing else would have much effect on his or the oak's polymeric skin. Soon even that would be overcome.

Jason left his chair and walked up to the large, panoramic window. Not much could be seen through the dirty cloud cover. Nevertheless, he looked up.

Not yet, he mused. Soon.

Soon the stars. *Homo Adaptus* could face just about any environment. Too hot, or too cold, or poisonous to most predictable life forms. The New Man could be subjected to stresses impossible for the *old* man, for Homo sapiens to survive. The old race would slowly die out. As painlessly as possible. As inevitably as a day following a long, obscure night.

Poor Jenny, he murmured.

***

The Eye
of the Hurricane

This must be what being dead is like. Silent, suspended in the middle of nowhere. I wish there were some noise. Any noise. I am surrounded by an impenetrable absence that fills the void of space to the brim. Some hours ago I could hear my own heartbeat. Now my ears filter out even that interference.

"God abides in the domain of stillness," a dog-collar told me, during my final goodbyes. Dog-collar, a priest who knew all the answers. I wonder how he knew. Had he been in out in space? On a long leash?

Now I too abide in total silence. Like God, only I'm not almighty. Not even powerful. Or all-knowing. And I can't take it anymore. I never realized silence could be so absorbing. So all-encompassing. So demanding….

Time minus 24 hours….

…and counting? Why didn't it say '*and counting*'?

At least, it could talk. It made a noise. A measured mechanical voice devoid of feelings or caring, which is what I feel like right now. Feelings are what you share. Here, there is no one. I wish the eggheads had given the computer a name like in all the good sci-fi movies. CPU doesn't sound very friendly. Doesn't sound like a name.

I switch one of the viewers over to Earth. Round and blue, and, well… just plain beautiful.

Ha, ha! Plain-beautiful, got it? Like pretty-ugly.

And tiny. Even in my powerful telescopic viewer, the Earth is so very, very tiny. Soon I wouldn't be able to see it at all. Maybe the eggheads were right. Maybe it was worth saving, though not for their sake.

The other viewer points straight ahead.

Wide lens.

Last week it showed a giant seashell gone wrong. Giant? About a hundred light-years across.

The Via Lactis, the Milky Way.

Not that I can see all of it. Just a fraction. The Canadian Indians saw it as a celestial turtle roiling the muddy currents of the Celestial River of Milk. Well, they were wrong. It looks more like a giant mollusk, a snail, spiralling its shell round its centre forever. Or like a hurricane seen from above, with a hole at its centre. Of course from my vantage point I could only see a small part of it. The centre—a mere 12.967 light-years wide.

A turtle?

I punched a few numbers. I was travelling at a constant acceleration of just over twelve Gees. Bit heavy but not too uncomfortable. The inertia stabilizers took care of that. The ship was doubling its velocity every... I'm no physicist. At this rate, I would leave the solar system within about ....

I punched the keys:

v = u+at, with 'v' being the final velocity, 'u' the initial, 'a' the acceleration, and 't' time. The question is what t gives v=2u? Hence

2u=u+at, so t=u/a. I know that a = 12G, so... with an initial velocity of say 20,000 km/hr, t would be u/12G

To hell with it. I don't really care.

The last I checked, we were escaping the Sol at approx. 270,000 kilometres an hour. That's faster than I can think. I lost interest. Whatever I worked out, the computer would overrule me. It would tell me exactly when I had to try the new engines. And hopefully they would work or there would be a big bang, and John H. Morton would be no more. Hell, it hadn't been a bad life.

God, I hate this silence. My life has been vibrant. Then this freezing....

"Talk to me, computer. What's your name?" I try.

"I am not programmed to answer this question, Commander."

I bet. Nor was my sixth wife just before she skipped town with that gigolo.

"What's his name, honey?" I like to know the name of the fellow I am about to kill. It's more personal that way. More friendly. "Take that, George!" Rather than, "Take that, you!" She, the sixth and last wife, got lost on a Caribbean cruise. Somewhere. How the hell do I know where? She's lost, isn't she? I wasn't even there.

Let me tell you, you can marry for love, or for convenience, but you can never, never marry just because you feel lonely. In the first case—you give, in the second you—share. In the lasts you just fake, or take... Well, what's-his-name took her. In fact, both of them. Good riddance.

Funny that... the moment she'd left I was no longer lonely. But, for a while, it was awfully quiet. Almost like in outer space....

Memories?

A steady drone reached me from afar and slowly filled every pore in my body. I could tell that sound anywhere...

The battered old, twin-engine WC-130 Hercules proudly upheld the tradition of the Hurricane Hunters. The good old Herk was over 35 years old but by far the best for the job. I had been chosen to fly into the eye of the storm. At the time people speculated what would happen when you got there, assuming you lived that long, but no one had actually flown right into the centre of the eye.

The two scientists and I were to be the first. For some unknown reason, I wasn't scared. Even trying to hold onto the stick while being tossed around like a kite in a gust of wind, seemed as natural here as if it were meant to be. Just like that. When you're twenty-seven, everything is fun. Only... you couldn't quite get enough of it....

I was quite proud of myself.
Then.

For the second time in my life, I would be the first man to breach the unknown. I expected the worst....

Time minus 23 hours....

I thought there's supposed to be silence here? And it's supposed to say *"and counting... "*

If only this was the old Herk....

The familiar Herk cockpit dissolved into a dozen tubes dangling from the ceiling. They were attached to various parts of my body and were intended to feed me barbiturates and other concoctions the moment the pain got too bad. They, the dreaded *them*, had to get by the "cruel and unusual punishment" rule. *Them*, the Justice Department. The judges and the executioners all rolled into one. That's why I'm here. In the void filled with silence. Anyway, I had no choice.

Actually, I did.

I could have taken triple life or the electric chair.

The chair would have saved the taxpayers' money. But, guess what? I've always been a sucker for adventure. As for my second option, I never suffered from a predisposition towards being fried. The smell would have been awful. I don't even like barbecues on the terrace. That was why I dropped my fifth wife. Actually, she dropped on her own—from the 42nd floor. Accidentally, of course. I told her not to barbecue with those gusts of wind, didn't I?

She landed two blocks away.

So—you've guessed it—I took life. Triple-life. But triple-life for a man barely sixty can be a long time. They freeze you for eleven months of every year, and thaw you for one, just to remind you that you're in jail. So you see, even at my age, triple-life is a *very* long time. And it's even worse now that life expectancy is about 150.

All thanks to genetic manipulation.

It was also by genetic manipulation that the eggheads produced the string of geniuses who, within a mere quarter-century, solved the problems of gravity, inertia, and some other problems associated with space travel, which I don't even begin to understand.

Oh, yes.

And they produced the first matter/antimatter

engine, which had to be tested. Enter *moi*. John H. Morton, the delinquent flier who strayed somewhere along the way. The fact is, that I did stray, mostly out of boredom. I took my personal skimmer under all the bridges over the Hudson River. I didn't make the last but one. Actually, I did, but some yo-yos had been banji jumping and I failed to give them due warning. They didn't make it. At least, not back to the bridge. For crying out loud, shouldn't have they learned to swim? I would have thought....

The genetically manipulated Einsteins were so smart, that there was little thinking, if any, left for mere mortals. I'd been thought of as smart in my day.

Now? I'm not even manipulated. Well, not much compared to them.

So how did I get in this mess, you ask?

I took a risk and three people died. It was not intentional, but the penalty was clear. Life. In fact, triple life. Not funny, but that's what the law said. So when they gave me a chance to test the M/A engines I said yes before I had time to think. I suppose I hadn't had much practice thinking, lately, what with my brain frozen most of the time.... It was only a month later, after a crash training-course, that I discovered that they had to test the engines outside the solar system.

OUTSIDE the Solar System!

Apparently, there was a small chance that the engine would start a chain reaction that would chew up our dear old sun with all the planets for dessert. When the mini big-bang was through, there would be a sort of void in space. Even the one hydrogen atom per cubic inch of space would be gone. Space was already about 600 billion trillion times less dense than water, yet, even so, the lone atoms would be gone. Some void! Only energy would be left. Some sort of static or potential energy, they said.

Or a big, fat nothing.

They said simply, "Plus atom and minus atom equals zero" This is what I am about a to become. Zero.

Anyway, so here I am, strapped to the biggest bomb ever built, trying to figure out how to kill time till the moment I push the button. Twenty-three hours from now, down there, on Earth, they will see a baby little nova blink in and out of existence and that would be that.

Aah, to be back on my Herk.

Those were the days.... It seems like only yesterday... *The engines revving, the wind tearing the crate apart... the eye of the hurricane way down, below...*

That was where my number two disappeared.

My second wife. Right in the centre of the eye. I watched her go down, ever so slowly…. Too slowly. We miscalculated the time needed for her decent. There is a strong updraft in the centre of the eye.

The eye shifted suddenly laterally.

She got caught …

Time minus 22 hours….

"Aw, shut up!"

"Yes, Commander."

As my fingers play over the computer's keys, the enhanced photo of Milky Way flashes on the screen. The similarity between a big hurricane and a spiral galaxy is uncanny. If I didn't know better, I'd quite easily mistake one for the other. Only at the centre of our galaxy there is a large, luminous halo. Hell, everything in space is large.

Gargantuan.

I couldn't see what was behind that halo. I could only imagine…. A hurricane has a hole at its centre. A hole of calm, as serene as a summer's eve. Sometimes the eye spans for some twenty miles and after the jostling and shaking we got in our trusty Herk, it was like being in heaven. Peace and serenity.

Peace and serenity in the eye of the storm.

Some said that the large halo was hiding a black hole. Black hole is a no man's land. It is private. Like being in love. Or like Calcutta. My fourth went to India on holidays and I never saw her again. Maybe I'm just unlucky? Anyway, human curiosity must end at its event horizon. Once you cross it, even if you could, you would be squashed like a gnat under an elephant's foot.

I've time to kill. I have to think about something?

I look at the screen. Spiralling around the galactic halo there are two sets of arms, winding their way towards outer space. We, our sun, are hanging some light-years outside the second spiral ring. We could never see the galactic centre from Earth because it's obscured by those two arms, as well as by the Great Rift—a cloud of dark dust. Actually, if you look towards Sagittarius with a half-decent telescope, you can see it. The Rift, not the Centre. Why is nature always hiding something from us? Just like my third....

Time minus 20 hours....

"What happened to 21 hours?"
"You told me to shut up, Sir."
Time sure flies when you're having....

Yeah....

Time.

Only usually time moves forward. It sort of gets bigger—the numbers do. Mine is shrinking. Sliding towards zero.

I dial a split screen, one showing a full-on view of the Milky Way, the other of my favourite hurricane, Pricilla. What strikes me again is not just the similarity but the beauty. The universe is like an ornament. Ornament of God? The ancient Greeks thought so. But if there is a parallel between the forces that shape the galactic and the hurricane configurations, then the galactic halo must be hiding a void. A place of tranquil nothing. A place as serene as a summer's day.... Isn't that what's supposed to happen to me if things go wrong?

I should be crying but all I can do is smile.

When they'd offered me the trip into the unknown, I thought they were kidding. I couldn't tell them that I'd had only one unfulfilled dream. Imagine, from a 1 x 1 x 3-meter box to Outer Space. I kept smiling. They almost cancelled me, suspecting that the freezing and the thawing affected my brain. After that, I kept a poker face whenever the eggheads were around. The rest of the time I would scream with joy.

I always loved astronomy.

When I wasn't doing stunts, like flying under the bridges, or sailing around the Tierra del Fuego horny protuberance, I gazed at the stars. It was really the sailing that did it. When you take the night watch, you are alone under the endless firmament.... It is so much vaster than when seen from the city. Vaster, yet I'd felt I could stretch out my arm and touch some of the stars. Later I'd learned that many of the diamonds I took to be stars were in fact nebulas and galaxies such as ours, and many much bigger than ours. Some were huge beyond imagination....

I dreamt of a river, a river full of stars.

The Arabs called it *Al Nahr*.

It was the River of Light to the Hebrews. The *N, har di Nur*.

The *Tien Ho* of the Chinese.

The Romans called it *Via Lactis*. Most mythologies coined their own names for it. For our home away from home.

Time minus five hours....

Sometime during my sleep, the computer must have opened the visors. Out here, there was no danger of colliding with any planetary debris. Not this far out.

Out here, millions of miles from a nearest town

or city, millions of miles from the nearest planet, our galaxy shone with the brightness of ten billion Suns. There are other galaxies, countless light-years away, that radiate with the brightness of ten trillion stars, and even more, ever more....

Giant nebulae, giant clusters and superclusters....

Each hiding deep, within its structure a single Eye; watchful, silent, attentive within the seeming chaos of the fulminating clouds, and gasses and rotating arms and globes and super globular giants. Some, creating new worlds, others cannibalizing less successful creations.... each and everyone spinning and rushing as though looking for something, for somewhere....

For someone?

Time minus four hours....

I shake my head. I feel drowsy.

Something funny is going on. It seems like minutes only since I took a nap. And now again my lids are heavy. Could they have put something in my drink? Were they pumping me....

...minus two hours....

For some reason, I'm still drowsy. Perhaps very

relaxed is a better word. The eggheads might be feeding me barbiturates from all those tubes hooked up to my body. But if they didn't want me on board at the critical moment, then why send me out here at all? On the other hand, all my reflexes are being radioed back to earth. Maybe that's all they want. Who can tell what the eggheads ever want? They don't live, they theorize. With all that genetic manipulation, I'm not even sure they're human.

"Computer, am I being drugged?"

"I am not programmed..."

"...to answer this question." I help it along. For some reason, it sounds almost human. "Go to sleep," I tell it.

"I am not programmed to sleep, sir."

No. Of course not. I could ask it what he's doing here, but he's probably not programmed to tell me. There, I said it. I said he not it.

I feel sluggish. Mentally sluggish.

There must be something about certain velocities. Man was not meant to travel at thousands of kilometres per second? Didn't Einstein say something about time and space being related in some way? I continue to drift off in some obscure directions; I am aware of my mind as though detached from my body. It regards the jewels of the universe from angles never seen by a human eye. I'm even detached from my mind. Or at least from my intellect. I'm becoming the perfect observer. Of everything. Or perhaps I just feel sated. As though I'd eaten the most sumptuous meal of my life.

Last super?

I smile again.

I realize that a smile took on permanent residence on my lips. I sense a strange sense of freedom, of utter independence—yet equally as strong is my sense of belonging. Here, out here, a million miles from anywhere, I am at home. Finally, I belong.

Beauty . . . such beauty....

I seem to be flying, side by side, accelerating with the missile that carries my body towards the galactic centre. Who knows what velocity the rocket is capable of? Who knows if laws of physics hold sway out here? If no one can hear the engines, do they work? Exist?

Beauty... such beauty....

Such silence....

Initiating the hundred-second countdown... 100 seconds...99... 98... 97... 96....

Who said that? Countdown? Ah… yes. Soon the matter-antimatter engines will flex their muscles. The positive and negative subatomic particles will annihilate each other. They will return whence they came. Energy never before witnessed will flood the space behind the spaceship. Are we allowed such frivolity with the laws of nature?

Why am I not worried?

...9...8...7...6...5...4...3...2...1...?

What happened? Why am I not afraid?

It was at this precise moment that, for the third time in my life, I discovered yet another Eye of the Hurricane. My whole life had been a twisted mass of disorganized forces, of gale force winds spinning their courses, swaying me this way and that, seemingly out of my control. Once again I recognized the power of Nature. The power of life. Even as the earthly hurricanes were to the galactic formations, so I was to an earthly hurricane. A minute universe struggling under the same laws. Drawing ever closer, falling, or being drawn, towards the centre of peace and serenity.

Towards the ever watchful Eye.

At the very centre of my being, at the core of that which I recognize as the seat of my consciousness, there is a field, neither defined nor limited by any geographical nor biological constraints... a field that remains ever steady.

In front of me sits Leila.

In all her beauty.

My one and only true love. The love I'd left in youthful foolishness. The love I've searched for the remainder of my life. At long last, It, the disembodied I, rests in supreme silence, in utter contentment. It is at peace with Itself, with Leila, as with Its universe, as with all Its forces gallivanting all around.

It rests in the serenity of a summer's eve...

***

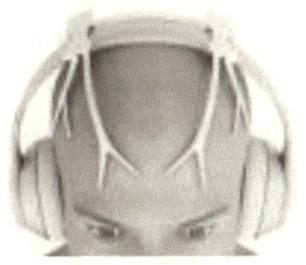

$\mathcal{D}$are

"Ah, Mr. Jones... back so soon?" Miss Barton smiled her standard civil-servant smile. I wouldn't be surprised if it was silicone, like certain other parts of her anatomy. For my part, I did my best to appear nonchalant, uncaring.

"Over four months since my eighty-percenter," I protested feebly. I suppose from her point of view I was a suicidal maniac. "I dropped in on a chance that you might have something exciting, Miss Barton," I continued hopefully.

They'd never warned us about the excruciating boredom of being immortal. That's right. Physically immortal. Whatever inadvertently happened to you, they either replaced it, re-attached it, or injected you with your own stem cells and your body took care of the rest all by itself. If that wasn't enough, nanobots, billionth-of-a-meter-sized robots, could be fed into your bloodstream to make appropriate adjustments. Believe me, immortality isn't all it's purported to be. I'd been stupid enough to sign up for it. That was... good God, that was a century ago! It seemed like a boon, at the time. Most of us did it. Now, most of us are queuing up at the doors of DARE. Hoping. Hoping for a temporary release from our congenital ennui.

My frustrations really hit me a few days after I'd turned 147. It wasn't a great age. Not by today's standards. But for a man who, to paraphrase Caesar, had been there, had seen it, and had done it, the routine began to weigh on me more and more heavily.

My last birthday party had alleviated my advancing ennui. Don't get me wrong. Jumping from one hot air balloon to another an inch below the stratosphere was not something I'd done before. It was fun. But the ever-present safety precautions had taken most of the thrill out of the experience. Ever since the accident back in 2093 when one young lady got tangled up in her own waist-long hair and smashed head first into a house killing three people inside, all skydiving was done with two reserve chutes. The young lady had been doing it for fun, but the people inside the house had been deprived of any thrill of expectation.

And that's what it was all about. The thrill of expectation.

"Expectations, my good man, is always greater than the fulfillment," the man had said signing me up for immortality. "You'll see," he'd added knowingly.

Actually, the man was Miss Barton's boss. Nice enough fellow, if you like a plastic smile wrapped in patent leather skin. I think they are all like that at DARE. Maybe they really are immortal.

Well, the expectations are greater than the fulfillment. I knew it was true, of course. If it weren't the case, people would never get married. Still, after I got rid of my seventh wife, I'd learned my lesson. But even the most dangerous stunts—other than marriages, I mean—stunts I'd performed 'just for the thrill of it', were never as good as what I'd hoped they might be. At least not until I registered with DARE. These guys were good. They really made you experience the thrill of dying. Well, almost....

DARE, they said, had been created by a group of people who provided you with a chance to 'almost' die. To kill yourself. At least, in 18 cases out of 20 with a margin of error of 3% points you had a 95% chance of killing yourself. The margins were necessary because suicide was still regarded as

murder and thus officially illegal. Imagine! Twelve
billion people, some of them over 200 years old, and
they still outlaw suicide. They say it's immoral.
Against human dignity. Boring people to death is
OK. And I suppose living in 10 square meters of
space is dignified! Fish enjoy more room in a village
pond than human beings in their assigned quarters.
To hell with the law!

I recall my first contact with DARE.

"You are Mister Frank Jones?"

"You have my file..."

"Yes, Sir." The young lady, who looked a young
thirty-going-on-eighty, thumbed through a folder and
then let her prosthetic fingers dance over the keys
with the speed of a bullet train. "I note that you are
new to us?"

"I read the rules, Miss Barton."

Actually, I hadn't, but I knew her name. It was
engraved in elegant letters in the front of her desk.
The *B* in *Barton* came in for an extra flourish. We all
needed some flourish in our life, I thought. The rule
she referred to was that you had to be 150 before you
were allowed to register with DARE. I'd made it by
three days.

"And what odds are you interested in, ah, Mr.
Jones?"

The most you could ask for was.

The whole thing was a put-up job, of course. DARE stood for the Department Affiliated to the Re-employment of Emeriti. Hogwash. It was all designed to get their hand on our retirement pensions. They kept a low profile. They didn't advertise except for a tiny blot on the Intertube. Nonintrusive. Somehow people ferreted them out. In their thousands. Still, I wonder why they kept such a low profile? Something to hide?

The vast majority of DARE customers were long retired. You can't employ 12 billion people when computers do 90% of the work. Can you? Anyway, who cares? If one could only die of boredom. Maybe that is what hell is like? You wait for death and it never comes. Never.

I looked up from my memories at Miss Barton's frozen features. She continued to stare at me with those large, limpid, washed out eyes. If I looked at her long enough I was sure I would have seen right through the back of her head. Maybe she was more like 130 going on 200. It was all the same to me. Time has so little meaning when you're immortal.

"Well, Mr. Jones?"

For a moment I hesitated. There is, always a chance of actually dying. Accidents do happen. Like in any extreme sport. Only this was premeditated. I wasn't really sure I'd had enough. Life, I mean. They were about to colonize Mars. They'd been talking about it for the last 100 years. Sure they had a few colonies there – living in cubicles even smaller than the ones down here on Earth and breathing re-cycled stinko. Not my idea of fun. Fifty years ago they said they would terraform the planet: turn into a replica of the one we've already polluted beyond recognition, but...? The Government makes lots of promises.

"95%," I said and let the air out of my lungs.

Two years ago, it had been different. Two years I also tried for 95%, only the pergameneous smile had said, "Sorry, Sir. On the first attempt, you are only allowed a 50/50 chance or less. These are the rules." She'd smiled an identical smile to the one she using right now. You've guessed it. A thin red smear across yellow wax split over artificially white teeth. Hadn't those people heard of plastic surgery?

"Can't you stretch the rules? I really am one-fifty, you know?" I recall having tried.

"Yes, Sir. I know. You are a young man. There may be a great future ahead of you."

"Fat chance..." I'd murmured under my breath. With 10,000 people competing for the same job? Fat chance. "I'm sure," I'd said louder. "50/50 it is then. When do I report?"

"We shall call you, Mr. Jones."

Blah, blah, blah. I'd tried arguing some more. It had been no use. DARE may be a secret organization but they sure acted like a government department. Rules, inflexibility, and red tape. They might as well work for the Government.

I forgot to mention. To take part in any DARE activity you had to be single. Divorced, widowed or whatever, but unattached. There was a reason for this. Although there was no payment for the services DARE rendered, you had to sign over your estate in their favour. If you didn't make it through your adventure, they kept whatever you were worth. After all, it's not as if you cared anymore.

Since that time I'd survived 60, 70 and 80% chances. Plus or minus 18 times out of 20 and all that. What I mean is that twice I needed some extensive repairs. The memories of the vivid experiences carried me for a few months at a time, but then the old boredom returned. There is only so much time you can spend watching the exploits of others. A TV on each wall didn't help. The experiences were still illusory. Phony. The artificial smells and noises pumped into my room didn't help either. Not any more. I knew I would have to go for broke. Sooner or later. It looked like it was going to be sooner. They say that a 95er can carry you for a year or two. Maybe longer. That the memories remain vivid. Each time I'd left for the DARE offices, I'd looked over my apartment for what could be the last time. Then I'd put on my breathing mask and leave for DARE. Hoping. Even hoping not to come back...

The first few times they'd been very clever recreating some of my memories from my youth and adding spice to them. They had to. With the additional experience of some 100 years, I was much too smart for my youthful pranks. Jumping Niagara Falls with protective gear was too easy. Doing so blindfolded added spice. Not with a bandanna but with drugs. I was as blind as a bat. They added similar quirks to my 60 and 70% chances also. But Niagara was the best. I thought my lungs would burst before I surfaced. Only when I was about to give up, I remembered a trick I'd learned in Tibet. A man with a beard longer then my arm taught me to hold my breath by reducing my heart beat. The Swami did it for 40 days. I made it for 4. Until the Niagara stunt, I'd forgotten all about it. I still remember the surprise on Miss Barton's face when she saw me a week later. I came in to sign some papers to revert my possessions back to myself. They were very honest about that.

"You have a tremendous will to survive, Mr. Jones," she said, disbelief in her eyes. She was thumbing through my file again. While in DARE' clutches, they had access to all your memories. Like a clone copy.

"Be that as it may, I'm ready for my ninety-five-percenter, Miss Barton. As ready as I'll ever be!" Why did I get the feeling that I wasn't expected to survive my previous stunts? Now that I think of it, I never seem to meet the same people in the queue. Funny that?

She pushed the usual disclaimer and some other documents across the desk. I signed them with total detachment, half wondering why I was doing this. I could go on with 60 or 70 percentages a while longer, but . . . the danger is addictive. It made me feel alive. It made me feel alive with an intensity that is quite unequalled in 'ordinary' life. In a strange way, it made you feel immortal. You were never so alive as when facing death. I was pitting my abilities against fate, against human ingenuity, against anything the world could throw at me. In a way, I was standing up against God Himself. And I still had a 5% chance of survival. A thin edge but... Somehow it was better than no edge at all. That would be suicide. A coward's way.

"You'll call me?"

She smiled that same septic smile. Or was it aseptic? It would be worth dying just so not to see it again. I spent the next two days tying up all the loose ends. Just in case. You never really believe you're going die. Not really....

***

I presented myself at the heliport at 10.00 hours, sharp. Two uniformed men whisked me to my destination. As usual, I had no idea what awaited me. A half-hour later more men in uniforms were squeezing me into what looked like a space-suit. I began getting excited. Space—The Final Frontier! I wondered what they had cooked up for me this time...

I'd never been to space. I would not be able to draw on any experience. I'd have to improvise. Sounded like fun.

"Take a deep breath, Mr. Jones. We have to add nitrogen to your blood to compensate for the difference in pressure," a woman's voice commanded.

The voice sounded familiar but I was too excited to play detective. I was about to take the highest survival test, with a 95% chance of not making it. I felt blood surging in my veins, and then, a wonderful sense of peace. I knew I could do it. Whatever it was.

The next moment I was led along a corridor and laid out on a flat surface that molded itself to the contours of my body. A pilot's chair, I presumed. Then vibrations stared. There was an array of twinkling lights all over the wall overhead. Or was it the ceiling? Then I felt stronger vibrations as at least three G's pushed my back.

"Lift off!" I said aloud.

For some minutes I couldn't move. Then, as though coming from a great distance, a steady, impersonal voice made an announcement.

"Welcome aboard, Commander Jones. A meteor fragment has struck the outer casing and the oxygen is seeping out. You have enough air in your space suit to last you 84.6 minutes. We regret to inform you that all the crew is unconscious and they cannot be revived on board. Their life is in your hands."

The voice was indeed impersonal and sort of androgynous. It could have been a man's or a woman's. Only it wasn't. It belonged to a computer's. A sort of HAL. I hoped it wasn't mad.

"I assure you, Commander Jones, that I am perfectly sane."

Commander?

"How did you know what I was thinking?" This was fascinating.

"My capacity to analyze your thought patters has

been programmed into my memory banks. I cannot read all your thoughts, but I can access the ones you are not consciously trying to hide from me."

So I do have some privacy, I mused. And then it struck me. "Why can't you land the ship yourself?"

"It would defeat the purpose, Mr. Jones. But I am at your disposal in all other respects."

The purpose? The purpose was to survive with a 95% chance against you. Against me. Christ! They don't pull any stops at the DARE. This experience must be costing them a small fortune. Perhaps a large one. No wonder they make you sign over all your possessions in their favour.

"I am not programmed to answer your concern," the voice droned.

"Never mind," I assured my circuitous friend aloud before I remembered that he could read my 'unguarded' ramblings. I wondered what thoughts I would wish to guard from him. It. From it.

"Where are we?"

"In three hours we enter lunar orbit. I can supply you with a number of suitable landing sites."

Three hours with 84 minutes of air. The DARE people must have remembered my surviving the Niagara dip. They'd upped the odds.

"Can you make the actual descent on your own?" I kept talking out loud. I felt foolish otherwise.

"I have the capacity to be programmed to do so..."

"But?" There had to be a 'but'.

"Very good, Commander, if I may say so. The 'but' relates to the code you must enter. And I am not programmed..."

"...to tell me what the code is." A computer with manners. A new one on me.

"That is correct, Commander Jones."

So that was that. Yet I had to find the 5% chance. It had to be hidden somewhere. Only where? My air wouldn't last, and the computer refused to cooperate.

"I shall land the ship on manual controls."

"Yes, Sir."

That's it? Yes Sir? What about "how do you land a bloody spaceship on a Lunar Base without ever having flown the tin-can before?"

"Very carefully," the voice offered impersonally.

I laughed. I was by now, maybe, some 82 minutes from death, but I had to laugh.

"Are you programmed to give me a quick course in landing spacecraft on lunar bases?"

"I can explain the functions of the dials overhead and the operational functions of the instruments in your armrests, Sir."

"Well?" I had 81 minutes left and HAL's cousin

was offering me theory.

"How long does it take to put this crate down on the moon? Once you get me to the orbit above the landing site, that is?"

"Assuming we are exactly in the right orbit, we'll need 37 minutes for the actual descent and for the lunar crew to connect us to the airlock."

If nothing else, the Big Brother was precise. Assuming he, I mean it, was right.

"Then you have exactly 44 minutes to teach me how to fly this heap."

The lesson was mostly digitized. I understood almost half of it. Then I took a deep breath and told the computer to wake me up 39 minutes before the countdown. As in Niagara, I slowed down my heartbeat and reduced my breathing to practically zero. The last couple of minutes before touchdown would be tough, but it couldn't be helped. My last thought was completely incongruous. I imagined that I saw Miss Barton's face framed in my spacesuit's visor. I entered the state of hibernation with a contented grin.

***

"I think that's about it?" Miss Barton also smiled as she leaned over and turned off the oxygen. There was no point wasting the precious commodity. Frank Jones's body was perfectly relaxed, his heartbeat was no longer detectable. After another 15 minutes, she removed his helmet and detached the synaptic connectors to the computer. The psychotronic computer programmed for empathetic responses had done its job. It responded to whatever Frank Jones wanted to hear. In fact, the whole plot had been written exclusively by the patient. The delinquent.

The one who dared.

Then with almost mechanical precision Miss Barton replaced the helmet over Frank's head and turned on the anesthetizing gas. After the Niagara experience, she wasn't about to take any chances. Mr. Jones had had more than his share of 'chances' already.

Her assistant, a man no more than a few years her junior, peered into Frank's visor.

"He looks so happy now, Miss Barton. I believe he's actually smiling."

Unbeknownst to them, Frank's brain, detached from the computer, was missing empathetic responses. It began searching for the tangible meaning of the reality in which he found himself. Slowly a gray haze began to cloud his vision. It seemed to spread over his dormant consciousness.

Smiling my foot. It's my lips that are smiling. Not me!

Don't they know that it's my body that's sedated but that my mind is perfectly conscious? And what the devil are they doing, removing my helmet in airless space? And how come they aren't wearing any helmets themselves?

"Turn off this stupid gas...!" I screamed. God, I screamed! But no voice would leave my mouth. And then I remembered: "I'm still in a hibernating state". It would take at least ten minutes to take conscious control of my body. At least ten minutes. And the anesthetic gas didn't help either. At least in my present condition, I'm hardly inhaling it.

"TURN OFF THAT BLOODY GAS!" I let out another silent scream only my mouth wouldn't open.

And then the strangest thing happened. I found myself floating in the air. The spaceship was gone. I was quite free... floating...

Miss Barton looked at Frank Jones' file on her desk. His last thoughts would be saved for record purposes. All part of research into the paranormal. But that was a different department. The lawyers and notaries would take care of the rest. Her job was virtually done. She had the satisfaction of doing an honest job. DARE was run by the Government to control, and if possible to reduce the population. It really was a top-secret department. At least its true function was. It was her job to assure that the Department Affiliated to the Retirees' Elimination had done its job in the most humane way possible. And the extra money didn't hurt either. They needed a lot for the new Martian colony and not many people paid taxes. How could they? They had no jobs...

I was beginning to get really woozy. Usually, my mind was at it's clearest in the state of hibernation. There were no sensual inputs to interfere with my thought-stream. The mind is a wonderful thing, left on its own. What a pity we misuse it so often.

Yet here and now, my usual clarity of perception was seeping away. I made one more attempt to tell them that I am perfectly conscious. They ignored me. Only my body is unconscious. MY BODY, I kept repeating. I am alive. ALIVE. Again I tried to scream but not even a whisper left my parched throat. Good-bye Earth. And... good riddance...

And then, quite suddenly, before I had a chance to get angry with Miss Barton and her cohorts, the darkness in my mind was replaced by a peculiar sunrise. A point of light grew through an omnipresent haze, like the rising sun seen on a spring morning over a distant lake. The light grew stronger until it filled my awareness to the exclusion of everything else.

What a glorious light...

"It's really wonderful how content he looks now," Miss Barton agreed with her assistant as she removed Frank's helmet for the last time. "Quite happy..."

Then she walked back to her desk and transferred Frank Jones' file to the 'retired' basket. Here, 'retired' carried a different meaning. With a satisfied grin, she began reprogramming the computer for the next 95%'er. Or 80 or even 50. All chances were exactly the same. Slim to nil. These days, all stunts were simulations. Good ones, she knew.

Then she checked the pressure in the tube supplying the hallucinogenic gas to the helmet. Her assistant removed Frank Jones' body to the holding area where it would be processed for recycling. It was all automatic, but checking the details herself made Miss Barton feel needed. Then she relaxed.

It was a good job, she thought, making people happy.

***

Black Hole

[Adapted from the Prologue to the *Gift of Gamman*]

I became vaguely aware of my surroundings when my body temperature reached 35.8^0 C. I remained quite still, eyes closed, the respirator filling my lungs with air rich in oxygen. Within the next few minutes, I became acutely aware of a prickly, painful consequence of blood forcing its way, with increased pressure, through the veins and arteries of my awakening body. Gradually, after a lengthy time of considerable discomfort, the thousands of dancing needles gave way to a sensation of profound sensual pleasure. My artificially maintained, previously greatly reduced, cardiovascular pressure was returning to normal. I felt alive.

Fairly alive. After a long, long time.

My breathing was becoming deeper, more

relaxed. The humming respirator sighed, hesitated, then turned itself off. I remained perfectly still, strangely afraid to open my eyes. Then, after a few more deep breaths, I peeked as if not knowing what to expect.

The cockpit, jet-black for nearly fifty years, now glowed with soft, gently diffused, greenish light. I must be giving a good impersonation of the Green Hulk—one of the ancient superheroes.

"Please don't make me angry..." I mused as if anything could. As if it would matter.

The light had been designed to lessen the impact on my half-dormant retinas. It took another few minutes for my optical nerves to focus. Then, few more for the mist to rise, the cobwebs of accumulated dreams, chimerical phantasms, to clear. From somewhere, far away, I heard a vaguely familiar voice.

"I am alive!"

The disembodied whisper was enunciating every syllable. "I am alive," I repeated softly, thinking that is was the most understated expression in the universe.

My voice sounded as though it belonged to someone who had just fought his way through the singing sands of the Sahara. I smiled wryly. Sahara desert—so many light-years away....

A slim indicator on my left told me that my body temperature has now reached 36.6°C. I glanced at the chronometer. The dial recorded 17,842th day since breaking Moon's orbit—about 49 solar years. Next, I looked at the gravimeter. The camera in front of me must have recorded an expression of surprise mixed with disbelief on my twisted, stiff, long stagnant features. I blinked repeatedly, refusing the evidence of my eyes. The gravimeter registered exactly 10 g's. Ten times the gravitational pull of the earth. The scientists back home had been right. I was still alive. The anomaly followed its own rules, obeyed its own laws. Had they been wrong, I would have had no one to blame. I, Adam Blake, Commander of the United Planets Federation, had volunteered for this mission.

I must have been crazy.

A few seconds later, automatically, the transparent polymeric cover of my berth slid silently over my head into the ship's bulkhead. Considering that I'd spent close to fifty years in suspended animation, my arms and neck manifested amazingly little stiffness. Not that I was about to go for a stroll. I grinned grotesquely, in appreciation. This lack of stiffness did not apply to my facial muscles.

"You've got to stop looking at the stupid mirror," I chided myself. The mirror was positioned just over my head. "To keep you company", the nurse had said. I called all the female engineers nurses. After all, their job had been to keep me healthy.

My mind shot back a few light years.

My once athletic body said nothing of the string of Ph.D.s in pure science as well as in various disciplines of ancient and modern philosophies I had acquired while waiting for some, as yet undefined mission. I had no way of knowing, when I would be assigned, to what task, on what expedition. Extra-solar treks were few and far between. Wherever they would send me, I'd hoped that, as a direct result of my broad spectrum of knowledge, my mind would retain the inquisitive freshness of a young man. Even now, at 36, ignoring the nominal ageing process during hibernation, under these unique circumstances, I prided myself at being able to take life as it came, meet it face on, without any preconceived ideas.

"You are an extremely resilient individual, Commander Blake, physically and mentally," Julie said yesterday, some fifty years ago. Lieutenant Julie was running the physio department. She'd been in her middle fifties. Then. Dear Julie. She must be dead by now.

I reached overhead and pulled on a thin plastic tube. By biting on it and sucking in quick succession,

I initiated the flow of a soothing liquid. Mostly glucose. Next, I pressed the 4th button to the left of the main console. Within two seconds, two brown biscuits of a reconstituted protein, carefully balanced with the three other dietary groups, popped up from a thin slot. I bit off a tiny piece. Almost instantly it distended itself, into a healthy morsel. Considering my protracted period of fasting, its taste was satisfying. During my hibernation, my body had been supplied with the necessary nutrients intravenously. This was different. This tickled my taste buds.

The slow chewing did wonders to my stiff facial muscles.

"I am alive," I repeated again. I noted that my voice began to resemble my normal, deep baritone. If anything could be referred to as normal, after fifty years of deep, very deep slumber. Fifteen minutes later I felt alert enough to inspect my ship.

The slim, cigar-shaped hull had not been designed for a return trip. The cockpit at the prow left no room for manoeuvring. Echoing my ancient predecessor, I travelled quite naked. All the physical exercise necessary to maintain my basic bodily functions had been provided by massage units built into my berth. A series of strategically placed electrodes, when activated, sent a microvoltaic current which contracted, held and released practically all the muscles of my body.

"It's a humanitarian concession," the nurse had said. She meant it was cheap enough not to break the mission's budget. Other than that, the ship was little more than an interstellar communication computer. My presence was almost incidental.

"Now don't start feeling sorry for yourself, lad," I said before I remembered that every word I uttered was recorded and automatically shot back at the Earth. "You volunteered, remember?" I added more softly.

The original rocket, behind me, had once measured over three hundred meters. When all the fuel necessary to arrive at the required velocity had been exhausted, the length of the hull had shrunk to a mere fraction of its former glory. Barely 19.8 meters, including the cockpit. Little more than a Moon shuttle. Virtually the whole space behind my exiguous quarters housed the nuclear generator, whose sole purpose was to sustain my life as long as possible. Officially. In a different reality, it served, principally, to provide the power necessary for the ship's laser communication system. As I'd mentioned, I'd been regarded as expendable; the data shipped back to earth—were not. They were *the* purpose of this one-way mission. I was there to enhance that purpose by personal observations. Assuming I survived any part of the trip. Or the hibernation, for that matter.

As for the personal reasons for the trip, since Joan and the children had died in the '16 Moon disaster, there was nothing to hold me back on Earth. Nothing at all.

The ship had no portholes anywhere. My eyes and ears to the outside universe consisted of a mass of gauges, dials, and six main colour screens, which provided visual and audio contact fore, aft and in the four remaining cardinal directions. As an added concession to my intellectual and emotional needs, the ship was equipped with a considerable library of fibro-optic memory storage units. Therein, a fair share of mankind's literary and musical heritage remained at my disposal. The eggheads, back home, had not been completely heartless.

"Must keep the lad happy, or he won't talk to us," I overhead a bald-head sniggering in the lab.

"Well, I still won't. I might talk to your children though," I said out loud. It was my turn to snigger.

In a nutshell, the ship had been designed as a missile that was to accelerate at a constant 1.67 gravities. The various stages of the rockets had been discarded, progressively, when empty. It had been hoped that by the time the impulse power runs out, I and the communication system would be trapped, or at the very least, within the influence of the gravitational field of the XM742 anomaly, commonly referred to as *the* Black Hole. They were hoping that I would have reached the Event Horizon—alive.

"And later…?" I would ask coyly.

This question had always succeeded in shutting them all up.

My mission had been preceded by years of arguments about uncertainty principle inherent in the quantum theory, particularly as regarding the emission of particles from the pulsars, the fast-spinning neutron starts, assumed to be the precursors of black holes. The obvious paradox had been settled, albeit hypothetically, by the theory postulating that the radiation originated not from the black hole itself, but from the 'empty' space, just outside the black hole's event horizon. Nevertheless, what had finally motivated the United Planets Federation to spend billions of dollars on expediting me towards and into the elusive non-space, had been the phenomenon of XM742. A series of independent observation satellites reported that light from a number of stars was noticeably bent around an invisible fulcrum, in the midst of the darkness of space. While the particle emissions from XM742 were relatively negligible, the photons refusing to follow their predestined path had been the determining factor. This discovery had mobilized armies of theoretical astrophysicists. Twenty-seven years later, ADAM ONE, had left the lunar orbit.

I had little reporting to do myself. The laser-oriented instrumentation transmitted, automatically, all the data that the sensors collected. It would continue to do so, up to that certain, as yet undefined point, whence the photons would no longer have the power to overcome the monstrous gravitational pull of the Black Hole. Assuming my cranium did not cave in onto the mushy grey matter it had been meant to protect, I was expected to add my own observations, a human touch, an insight, into the unknown characteristics of the anomaly.

I glanced overhead and I touched my cranium to make sure it was still there. Mirrors can be misleading.

Within a very short time, the gravimeter advanced a few decimal points towards the 11g mark. I knew that the gravitational field increased exponentially to the distance from my objective. A paradox. Subjectively, I remained in zero gravity. Observed from an astrophysical distance, an anomaly, such as XM742, appeared to generate a directional, gravitational pull, as indeed it did, within a vast radius of influence. A black hole's horrendous gravitational attraction might vary from a few parsecs, to tens of thousands of light-years. The hub, the very centre of a galactic core, might well hide a prodigious anomaly, exacting its majestic, gravitational influence so great as to hold hundreds of billions of stars in its flamboyant grasp. Once within the space matrix distorted by its influence, its event horizon, the theoreticians theorized that space would have been distorted sufficiently for the gravity to act as a field rather than a directional force.

So much had been predicted, suspected, assumed. At the home base.

To understand my own predicament, I drew an analogy with the theory of the expanding universe, which holds that every major star cluster, every galaxy, is moving away from every other such system. Within the space distorted by the anomaly, however, a partial reversal took place. While the laws governing the expanding universe tended to pull solid objects apart, or, at the very least, away from each other, the intense gravitational field of the anomaly provided the reverse motive. Such a resultant singular field could be expected to hold every atom in perfect, if delicate or precarious equilibrium in relation to every other atom.

This effect had been suspected at the home base, if only within the peripheral behaviour of the anomaly. If they were right, I would confirm their reasoning by merely staying alive. A little longer...

I grinned at the mirror overhead.

"I'm alive!" I repeated again as if this fact was reason enough to give my life in exchange for new knowledge. I did not regard myself as a hero. I'd competed with many young astronauts for the privilege of taking part in this unique experiment. I'd won the privilege to venture into the unknown. To boldly go where no man....

No sane scientist dared to even speculate what enigmatic laws, gargantuan forces, or fields, secrets and paradoxes, governed reality near the centre of a black hole. Let alone one wielding the effect of XM742.

"Space is bent upon itself. Completely!" one genius had announced. "It's inverted, I tell you," claimed another. The consequences of such hypotheses, however, were beyond the scope of human imagination.

I smiled at my reflection when I realized that on Earth, under my present conditions, my body would weigh over 800 kilos!

"And you ain't seen nothing yet, kiddo!" I said

out loud.

Suddenly, I felt light-hearted. Once again I forgot that every word I uttered was instantly converted into laser impulses and transmitted at 300,000 kilometers per second, towards base. Fifty years into the future, countless solons would analyze each word, each syllable, probably mystifying over the depth of my statement. I must have been the only human being within a good few light years, who found my predicament funny. I roared with laughter.

"Poor lad," I could hear the eggheads of the future. "He'd lost it..." There would be nodding of heads, perhaps a surreptitious tear. I laughed some more.

On finishing my second biscuit, I performed all the routine checks and reported AAA to whoever was, or rather will be, listening.

"I wonder who they are... what they look like..." I mused aloud. I had to. Hearing my own voice kept me human. Or just sane. There was no one else in the vicinity....

Back home, many of my friends, colleagues, must have already died. From old age. The rest of them would be dead by the time any of my transmissions reach Earth. How ephemeral is human existence... For a moment, I grew pensive. I dialled

Mozart. One of the screens displayed a complete selection of Mozart's works. I punched 'Don Giovanni'. I needed something amusing, irresponsible, and Leporello footed the bill. The hapless servant of the exacting rogue never failed to make me laugh. The overture filled the cockpit. A little later, a tiny, holographic stage shimmered, then solidified, just over a meter away, directly in front of my eyes. Though the human figures were no more than ten centimetres high, each seemed perfect in every detail.

After the first act, I glanced at the chrono. The time registered 17,842.79. "Bloody nonsense!" I shook my head. I punched CHRO and then the code for the elapsed time since I'd been 'reactivated'. The dial now read 0.1284 ET. I could reset the Elapsed Time chrono whenever I wanted. For whatever reason.

"That's better", I smiled with satisfaction, "just over three hours." The gravi climbed to 11.89.

I closed my eyes and lost myself in the music. I knew the scene by heart. *Il Commendatore* of Seville was just inviting Don Giovanni to hell. I wondered where I was going.

At 1.729 ET I pressed for another biscuit. This time a fresh salad taste tickled my palate. I washed the 'salad' down, with a near perfect taste of white Burgundy. "Cheers," I gurgled raising my empty hand. The same tube provided an excellent facsimile of black coffee.

I lowered my console, stretched out and pressed the relax button. My berth began vibrating. A pleasant, almost seductive, undulating motion. Within ten seconds I fell asleep. The moment my brain began emitting alpha rhythms, all the dials, screens and coloured buttons went black. Black as the blackness of outer space. They say that God abides in the deep silence of our hearts. He must also abide in space.

The endless silence of deep space.

While I slept, various sensors continued to monitor my physiological responses. The same instant the data were transmitted towards Earth. My diet had been designed to induce maximum hours of sleep. No one at home base could have guessed how long the 'star' fall would take. Sleep had been regarded as the best means of preserving my sanity. Should anything unforeseen happen during my rest period, I would be instantly awakened. If necessary, the drug in the coffee would be counteracted through a permanent intravenous implant grafted under my left knee. Permanent? I slept like a newborn baby. After all, I'd earned it. This was the first *real* sleep I enjoyed in almost fifty years!

At 2.73ET, the electro-mechanical massage started. At 2.8 I was awakened. The moment I regained control over my senses, I looked at the gravimeter. For the second time since reactivation, I challenged the evidence of my eyes. It never crossed my mind to question the efficacy of the instrumentation. The dial reported 74.89 g's.

"My God!" I muttered, "I shouldn't be here. At least not in one piece!" Almost instantly my momentary horror gave way to condemned man's humour. "Or at least, in a much, much smaller piece..."

Three sleep cycles later, at 17,000 g's, it became apparent, that within this incredible environment, the centrifugal forces maintained the individual particles of matter in a superb, quantified, equilibrium. My ship was no longer subject to the established laws of the expanding universe. It responded to a field where perfect harmony prevailed, defying the principally directional forces governing the space left behind. As each individual atom, each subatomic particle that could be quantified became subjected to the fantastic stresses, they each contracted within their own, individual orbit of existence or activity, while the concentric acceleration continued to increase their mass. The result was that as the mass increased, the nuclei shrank further and further apart. Each quantum collapsed in, upon itself, while its mass grew, exponentially, towards infinity.

A Paradox, a Singularity, a Black Hole within— yet without the universe. Are there not parallel universes all around us?

I spent the next few waken periods pondering the possible consequences of such conditions. Finally, with considerable trepidation, indeed, stretching my courage to the outer limits, I decided to test my theory.

I extended my hands at arms length. Then, joining my palms I began pressing them together. The next instant, I witnessed the seemingly impossible. My stomach fought its own battle to retain its state of balance. And biscuits.

You must never be sick in a free fall.

Never! My mind, demanding, screaming for a familiar point of reference recoiled in horror. The sensation was that of immersing my hands in wet sand or a bucket of ready-mix concrete. Only there was no sand or wet concrete. Not within fifty light years. By an effort of sheer will, I increased the pressure. My palms began to merge into each other and then reappear on opposite sides.

When I pulled my hands apart, my mouth and throat felt arid. I glanced at the mirror. In perverse contrast, fresh beads of perspiration formed on my forehead. I suddenly realized that during the feat I just performed, I experienced absolutely no pain. Nevertheless, I did not dare to wipe my forehead, lest my hand penetrated my own skull. I lay back exhausted.

My suspicions were right, as were those of the more audacious theoretical physicists' back home. Here, reality no longer obeyed the laws of our universe.

Would this knowledge be communicated to Earth? Ever? Or did the universe extract the ultimate penalty from all who reached out, who dared to penetrate its inner, arcane secrets?

The ship now travelled within a few decimal points of the speed of light. There was no sensation of motion. Absolutely none. The four digital gravimeters, running sequentially like puny electric meters back home, were all working overtime. Only a blur on the first three dials testified that they were still working. Incongruously, I became acutely aware of the advantages of electronics systems. Had the gravis been designed with rotating needles, they would have, long ago, merged into their surrounding casing.

During the time taken by my experiment and the subsequent effort at regaining sanity, the g's had climbed to 22,600. Even as I watched, spellbound, the dial climbed faster than I could count.

23,000....24,000....26,000....29,000....

Such figures, numbers, concepts, no longer held any rational meaning!

Why am I still alive?

What is life?

What is reality?

What am I?

Time and motion merged into the same category. I lay back, inert, silent, rapidly losing awareness of my physical body. At 35,000 g's, I no longer retained any perception of pulmonary or cardiovascular activity. Yet, evidently, I occupied the same space in the same cockpit. As I directed my attention to my body—it seemed to vibrate with a slight shimmer. I 'saw', though hardly with my optical senses, that the space occupied by my body consisted of countless billions of shining, spinning, constantly oscillating points of light.

"Stars", I thought, in abject wonder. "I am a galaxy of stars held together by an act of my will. The substance of my body is moving, acting, functioning, and behaving in direct relation to my imagination. Whatever I imagine—must follow."

As if to prove the point, I pictured himself

outside my own ship. Within a split second, I was looking at the hull, myself hovering nearby, suspended in a dark grey emptiness. Strangely calm, I thought of my physical body. The hull of the ship became instantly transparent. Inside, reclining in total repose, I regarded my own body.

"I accept as reality whatever I perceive with my senses," a thought formed in my mind.

"What senses?" someone asked.

"Where am I?"

"Who?"

I was acutely aware that the capacity of my consciousness was expanding in direct proportion to my ability to absorb it. The next thought placed me back in my reclining body, though I no longer felt its limitations nor depended on it for my self-awareness.

My thoughts drifted to my past. Rather than becoming aware of Adam Blake, the astronaut, my mind showed me a sequential kaleidoscope of incidents, seemingly spanning millions upon millions of years. I saw myself as a rudimentary consciousness embodied in various animal forms. A flash of light brought me into a two-legged creature. Hairy, primitive. Proud? My mind registered a critical difference from my previous states of awareness. The animal form I now occupied registered a spark of self-awareness. The first spark. It possessed an embryonic concept of 'I am'. My mind examined various stages of my own growth. I perceived a slowly emerging, very gradual, yet distinct pattern. Suddenly I knew. I understood the evolutionary process. It was as though all that had ever happened to me manifested the implicit purpose of driving me relentlessly to this present moment. Nothing, not one single event in the eons of my existence occurred without reason. Each cause had its effect. Every effect was preceded by a cause. The essence, the sum total of the relationship between my growing awareness and my personal, individual environment, was an intractable, obstinate tendency towards a state of balance. Towards order.

Balance, harmony, equilibrium.

Beauty.

My mind reached out to the stars. As my attention left my own, puny pattern, I sensed a similar matrix in the universe around me. It was no longer a physical entity. Yet the patterns, the forces at play, all had their effects in energy and matter. The earth, the solar system and the most distant galaxies were all suspended in a single lattice of intergalactic forces. No part had more importance than any other. Each served its predestined purpose, its predestined position, in the balanced state of the unified field of forces. An atom, a molecule, a speck of dust, a rock, an asteroid or a planet; they all meshed smoothly into the Pattern. Even as the subtle, harmonious vibration held them together and imbued them with life, with the individual existence, so the light was akin to knowledge, to awareness growing, expanding towards the final effect, towards the universal interplay of the primeval forces.

I sensed the mystery of eternal becoming. My mind watched, absorbed. Through it, I witnessed the birth of countless stars, as the vast clouds of gases had been ignited into convoluting, focal centers through which light entered and distributed energy necessary for the next step on the endless journey of destiny and fulfillment.

Then, even as a tsunami sweeps everything in its path, my mind, fired by an overwhelming realization of purpose, was flooded with a single, all-exclusive, desire.

I needed to be one with this glorious pattern. I needed to unify all forces within my own being into a singular state of total awareness.

My awareness hovered at the very edge of the space-time continuum.

In an endless ocean of absolute, intense darkness, a single point of light commanded my attention. As the light swelled, increased in magnitude and intensity, I continued shedding the remnants of my mind. I was becoming one with that which I perceived. Within seconds or aeons, beyond time or space or any limitations, the light source grew, augmented, distended, until it burst with such ferocity that billions upon billions of suns could not rival its brilliance.

The blaze filled, penetrated, overwhelmed, the deepest recesses of my consciousness. Burning, destroying, liberating in a cathartic orgy. Nothing, nothing existed but pure, white essence of light. The essence of the undifferentiated, unfulfilled infinite potential of all Knowledge. All Power. The single Unifying Force of the yet unmanifested universes. It was the Light that was, that is, that forever will be.

Within that single instant of realization, I, Adam, or the consciousness which had once defined Adam, became one with the blaze around me. I was no longer within it, nor part of it. I was the Light Itself.

I AM   I AM   I AM   I AM I AM IAMIAMIAMIAM sang a single atonal vibration, so fine and pure as to enfold infinity with aliquot harmonics. It held, sustained and glorified the essence of my being.

I AM, it reverberated in a limitless glory of pure consciousness.

I AM the birth, the sustenance and the fulfillment

I AM the source of all knowledge

I AM the power of my own being

I AM life itself

I AM

Adam Blake chose to return to earth four decades after he had been sent on his unique mission. His return was as easy, as his departure—difficult. Just as Black Hole satisfied the centripetal laws of the universe, so his own sun, like every other, served as a focus for the centrifugal emission and distribution of Life energy. Adam did not have to come back. In fact, Adam no longer existed. He gave his life in order to gain Life. This fact alone liberated him from the need of assuming, once again, a human form. Yet, as it sometimes happens, he chose to return. He wanted to help those who were ready, though not lucky enough, to have been selected for his last, his one-way mission.

At a particular a fragment of eternity, a young, healthy, proficient pilot was falling to his death from an exploding airplane. The ejection seat worked, but the parachute failed to open. As the pilot's consciousness vacated the falling body, Adam, or that

that had once been Adam, entered the vacant flesh and brought it gently to the ground. No one witnessed the accident. He discarded the useless parachute, straightened his uniform examining its content.

"I'd chosen well," he murmured as he smiled at the familiarity of human form, "it might have been made for me," he nodded knowingly.

He then looked around. The Earth hadn't changed. The sky was blue, the grass as green beneath. Welcome back, the wind whispered in the nearby trees. A bird whistled a paean while diving over his head. "Why thank you," he whistled back, "I love you too."

The next day, John Galt, for that was the name of the body that Adam had entered, reported the accident to his superiors. He failed to mention just one pertinent detail. He did not mention that his parachute did not open.

"John Galt reporting for duty," he said.

The malfunction in the ramjet's engine design was readily corrected.

Six years later, John Galt was promoted to Commander, the rank he'd held as Adam Blake. A year later he was transferred to Moon Base. He arrived just in time to help the colony of scientists decipher the endless string of data, arriving from a relatively primitive spaceship, falling, relentlessly, into a strange phenomenon known as the XM742 anomaly.

John Galt knew it as the brightest Black Hole in the Universe.

***

Acknowledgments

I would be remiss were I not to thank my many friends who have read the galley proofs and helped to make this anthology a success. Most especially my thanks go to those who have read and offered me their reviews. Also, their diligent editing raised this anthology to an acceptable literary standard. Finally, my gratitude to my wife, Bozena Happach, who put up with being a grass widow for weeks on end and then allowed me to benefit from her insights.

Sincerely,
Stan I.S. Law

A Word about the Author

Stan I.S. Law (aka **Stanislaw Kapuscinski**), architect, sculptor, and prolific writer, was educated in Poland and England. Since 1965 he has resided in Canada. His special interests cover a broad spectrum of arts, sciences and philosophy. His fiction and non-fiction attest to his particular passion for the scope and the development of Human Potential. He authored more than forty books, twenty of them novels. His short stories, 'literary', though tending towards Visionary-Science-Fiction, have been published extensively.

Under his real name, he published twelve non-fiction books sharing his vision of reality. He also composed two collections of poems in his original native tongue in which he satirizes his view of the world while paying homage to Bozena Happach's sculptures.

If you enjoyed these stories,
*please, write a (brief) **review** on Amazon.*
Thanks.

The anthology continues in Sci-Fi Series 2

And again, if you enjoyed both collections
and were kind enough to have written reviews
wherever you could, you can continue to enjoy Stan
Law's imagination in twenty, full-length (including
two Science Fiction) novels.

By the same author

Trilogies
(ebooks only)
ALEXANDER TRILOGY
AVATAR TRILOGY
AQUARIUS TRILOGY
WINSTON TRILOGY

Novels

MARVIN CLARK—In Search of Freedom
ONE JUST MAN [Winston Trilogy, Book One]
ELOHIM [Winston Trilogy, Book Two]
WINSTON'S KINGDOM [Winston Trilogy, Book Three]
THE AVATAR SYNDROME [Avatar Trilogy Book One]
HEADLESS WORLD [Avatar Trilogy Book Two]
AWAKENING—Event Horizon [Avatar Trilogy Book Three]
THE PRINCESS
ALEC [Alexander Trilogy, Book One]
ALEXANDER [Alexander Trilogy, Book Two]
SACHA—The Way Back [Alexander Trilogy, Book Three]
YESHÛA—Personal Memoir of the Missing Years of Jesus
PETER & PAUL [Intuitive Sequel to YESHÛA]
THE GATE—Things My Mother Told Me
NOW—Being &Becoming
ENIGMA OF THE SECOND COMING
THE GIFT OF GAMMAN
WALL—Love, Sex, and Immortality [Aquarius Trilogy Book One]
PLUTO EFFECT [Aquarius Trilogy Book Two]
OLYMPUS—Of God and Men [Aquarius Trilogy Book Three]

Short stories
THE JEWEL
CATS & DOGS
SCI-FI SERIES 1
SCI-FI SERIES 2

Poetry in Polish
KILKA SŁÓW I TROCHĘ GLINY
WIĘCEJ SŁÓW I WIĘCEJ GLINY
(temporarily out of print)

Non-fiction
Stanislaw Kapuscinski
(aka Stan I.S. Law)

KEY TO IMMORTALITY
[Commentary on the Gospel of Thomas]
BEYOND RELIGION
Volumes I, II and III
[Collections of Essays on Perception of Reality]
DICTIONARY OF BIBLICAL SYMBOLISM
An Indispensable Tool for the Understanding of the
Hidden Meaning of Scriptures
VISUALIZATION—Creating your own Universe
DELUSIONS—Pragmatic Realism
VICIOUS CIRCLE
In Search of Secular Ethics
[ebooks only Volumes 1-5]

INHOUSEPRESS

Montreal, Canada